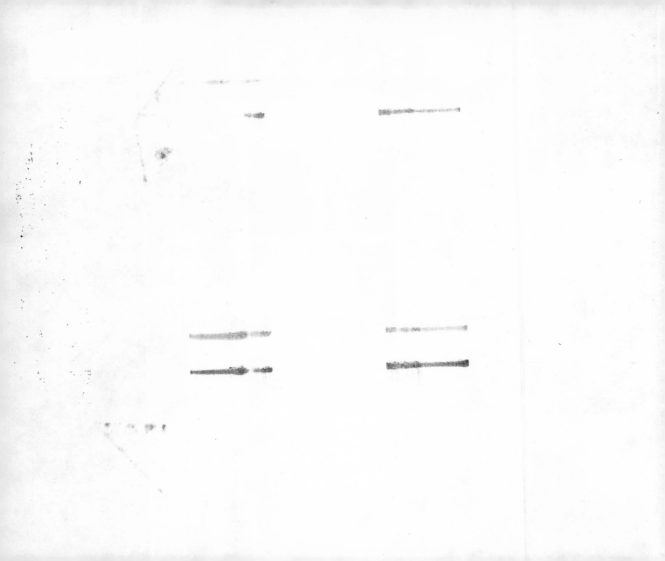

THE ROOM
Mordicai Gerstein

Harper & Row, Publishers

For my father
Samuel

E
GER
C. 1

The Room
Copyright © 1984 by Mordicai Gerstein
Printed in the U.S.A. All rights reserved.

Library of Congress Cataloging in Publication Data
Gerstein, Mordicai.
   The room.
   Summary: An artist re-creates the many characters
from years past who have lived in the room that is
once again for rent.
   [1. Dwellings—Fiction]   I. Title.
PZ7.G325Ro 1984   [E]   83-47709
ISBN 0-06-021998-X
ISBN 0-06-021999-8 (lib. bdg.)

1 2 3 4 5 6 7 8 9 10
First Edition

This room is for rent.
It's full of sunlight all day long.

Many years ago it looked like this.

A young couple moved in.
They played music together.

Their baby was born in this room.

They had big birthday parties.

The baby grew up and moved away
to become a cowboy.

The couple grew older and got a pet rabbit.

When the old couple moved to a warmer climate,
two sparrows flew in.

They raised a sparrow family.

One evening, a mother and father
and their little girl moved in.
The father was in the fur business.

The sparrows moved out. The little girl
saw them leave and thought they were fairies.

An uncle came to visit the little girl.
He told stories of sailing to Iceland.
He gave her a toy ship.

A month later, they all packed up
and sailed to Iceland.

A mysterious person rented the room
and planted a pear tree near the window.
The pears were wonderful.

When the person moved away, mysteriously,
a dressmaker moved in. She had too many cats.

A real king and queen came to dinner once. They lived
in a palace with too many mice. They invited the dressmaker
to come with her cats and live with them. She did.

Then a family of acrobats moved in.

When they joined a traveling circus,
a plumber moved in. He collected kites.

When he left, twins who were bank robbers
used the room for their hideout.

The police came and arrested them.

A dentist who loved ducks moved in.

One day, an old woman came and asked to see
the room. She said she used to live there
before she moved to Iceland.

They had tea, and she told him how she had seen
some fairies fly out the window when she was
just a little girl.

Next, a band of Irish musicians rented the room
and played day and night.

The neighbors complained, and they had
to move out.

A family of artists moved in.

When they left, the landlord had
the place repainted.

A magician moved in and did incredible tricks
that no one saw, except a little boy next door.
He peeked in the window.

One day the magician disappeared with all
his equipment.

The room is for rent again.
It is full of sunlight all day,
and the pears are wonderful.